Highlights **Puzzle Readers** | LEVEL **1** LET'S EXPLORE READING

Maggie and Pie
and the Cookie Contest

By Carolyn Cory Scoppettone
Art by Paula J. Becker

HIGHLIGHTS PRESS

Honesdale, Pennsylvania

Stories + Puzzles = Reading Success!

Dear Parents,

Highlights Puzzle Readers are an innovative approach to learning to read that combines puzzles and stories to build motivated, confident readers.

Developed in collaboration with reading experts, the stories and puzzles are seamlessly integrated so that readers are encouraged to read the story, solve the puzzles, and then read the story again. This helps increase vocabulary and reading fluency and creates a satisfying reading experience for any kind of learner. In addition, solving puzzles fosters important reading and learning skills such as:

- shape and letter recognition
- letter-sound relationships
- visual discrimination
- logic
- flexible thinking
- sequencing

With high-interest stories, humorous characters, and trademark puzzles, Highlights Puzzle Readers offer a winning combination for inspiring young learners to love reading.

This is
Maggie.

This is
Pie.

Maggie and Pie love to cook.
But sometimes Maggie
gets a little mixed up.

You can help by
using the clues
to find the supplies
they need.

"The pot holders are with the oven mitts.
The pot holders are square.
The oven mitts look like mittens.
Both are yellow with blue dots.
Can you find them?" asks Pie.

Happy reading!

3

4

The sun shines on the big tent.

"I am so excited for the contest!"
says Maggie.

"I am, too!" says Pie.
"Look! There is our table."

"It is next to that pretty garden,"
says Maggie.

"Teams, it is time to start,"
says Mrs. Baker. "Ready, set, GO!"

"First, we mix up the salt
and the baking soda," says Pie.

"I can do it," says Maggie.

"Oh no," sighs Pie.

"We mix up *our* salt

and baking soda in a bowl."

"Why didn't you say that?"

asks Maggie.

"Next, we add the flour.

It is in a yellow bag.

It is on the top shelf.

It is not the smallest bag.

Can you find it?" asks Pie.

"Here is the flour!" says Maggie.

"Thanks," says Pie.

"Now we take butter and sugar, and beat."

"I can get them," says Maggie.

"Here are the butter and sugar,"
says Maggie. "And here is the beet."

"Oh no," sighs Pie.
"We beat the butter and sugar
with a mixer."

"The mixer is on the bottom shelf.

It is silver and white.

It is next to the teapot.

Can you find it?" asks Pie.

13

"Here is the mixer!" says Maggie.

"Now we need a baking sheet," says Pie.

"I can get it," says Maggie.

"I could not find a sheet.

Will this work?" asks Maggie.

"Oh no," sighs Pie.

"The baking sheet is on the rack.

It is purple.

It is flat.

It is on the shelf under the pots.

Can you find it?" asks Pie.

"Here is the baking sheet!"
says Maggie.

"Thanks," says Pie.
"Now we scoop the dough
onto the baking sheet in rows."

"Here is a rose," says Maggie.

"But where does the dough go?"

"Oh no," sighs Pie.

"We line up the scoops in *rows*."

"Next, we need pot holders," says Pie.

"I can get them," says Maggie.

"Pie," Maggie calls.

"Look what a good job
our pot holders are doing!"

"Oh no," sighs Pie.

"The pot holders are with the oven mitts.

The pot holders are square.

The oven mitts look like mittens.

Both are yellow with blue dots.

Can you find them?" asks Pie.

"Here are the pot holders!"
says Maggie.

"Thanks," says Pie.

DING!

"Can we eat the cookies now?"
asks Maggie.

"Not yet," says Pie.

"We need to decorate them first."

"I can do it," says Maggie.

"Okay," says Pie. "I will clean up."

"Three, two, one . . . STOP!"

says Mrs. Baker.

"Teams, please bring us your cookies."

"You all made wonderful cookies," says Mr. Baker.

"The Yummy Cookie Prize goes to Flo and Mango," says Mrs. Baker.

"The Pretty Cookie Prize
goes to Penny and Gwen,"
says Mr. Baker.

"And the Surprise Cookie Prize
goes to Maggie and Pie,"
says Mrs. Baker.

"Do you know what I like more than baking cookies?" asks Maggie.

"What?" asks Pie.

"Eating cookies!" says Maggie.

Beet Cookies

MAKES ABOUT 30 SMALL COOKIES

ADULT: Wash, peel, and dice the beet into cubes. In a large pot, cook beet cubes in boiling water for 10–15 minutes until soft, then drain. Puree the cooled beet cubes in a food processor or blender.

Wash your hands!

What You Need

- ½ cup unsalted butter, softened
- ¼ cup sugar
- ½ teaspoon vanilla
- 1 teaspoon orange zest (optional)
- 1 beet
- 1 cup flour
- Pinch of salt
- Parchment paper

1. Beat.

ADULT: Preheat oven to 325°F.

Beat the **butter** and **sugar** in a mixer until light and creamy, about 3 minutes.

2. Mix.

Stir in the **vanilla, orange zest,** and 1 tablespoon of the pureed **beet**. Slowly add the **flour** on low speed and mix until thoroughly combined.

3. Chill.

Cover and refrigerate the dough for at least 30 minutes.

4. Roll.

On a floured surface, roll out the dough to about ¼ inch thick. Cut the dough with a cookie cutter or an upside-down glass. Place the cookies on a baking sheet lined with **parchment paper** at least 1 inch apart.

ADULT: Bake 10–15 minutes until the edges begin to brown.

No rolling pin? No problem! Just roll the dough into a long log, and then cut slices.

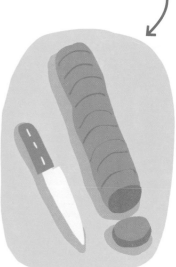

For information about permission to reprint
selections from this book, please contact
permissions@highlights.com.

Published by Highlights Press
815 Church Street
Honesdale, Pennsylvania 18431
ISBN (paperback): 978-1-64472-694-5
ISBN (hardcover): 978-1-64472-695-2
ISBN (ebook): 978-1-64472-696-9

Library of Congress Control Number: 2021950408
Printed in Melrose Park, IL, USA
Mfg. 03/2022

First edition
Visit our website at Highlights.com.
10 9 8 7 6 5 4 3 2 1

Recipe by Casey Zier, Be Kind Bake House

LEXILE®, LEXILE FRAMEWORK®,
LEXILE ANALYZER®, the LEXILE®
logo and POWERV® are trademarks of
MetaMetrics, Inc., and are registered
in the United States and abroad. The
trademarks and names of other companies and
products mentioned herein are the property of their
respective owners. Copyright © 2022 MetaMetrics,
Inc. All rights reserved.

For assistance in the preparation of this book,
the editors would like to thank Julie Tyson, MSEd
Reading, MSEd Administration K–12, Title 1 Reading
Specialist; and Gina Shaw.